KU-151-794

A TALE OF TWO CITIES

CHAPTER One   *Brought back to life* 5

CHAPTER Two   *The Trial* 10

CHAPTER Three   *Death in the Countryside* 14

CHAPTER Four   *A Terrible Secret* 18

CHAPTER Five   *Desperate Days* 23

CHAPTER Six   *Revolution!* 27

CHAPTER Seven   *A Prisoner* 31

CHAPTER Eight   *No Hope* 34

CHAPTER Nine   *The Secret Letter* 39

CHAPTER Ten   *Number Twenty-three* 44

Introduction

Charles Dickens was born in 1812, the second of eight children. When he was twelve years old, his father went to prison because he owed money. Charles went out to work to help his family. He never forgot this terrible time when he was poor, and later used his experiences in some of his stories.

In his twenties, Charles found work writing about London life for newspapers and magazines. Some of these articles were published as a book called *Pickwick Papers*. This is how Charles Dickens became famous at the age of twenty-four.

A Tale of Two Cities was published in 1859. The two cities are London and Paris. It tells the story of Doctor Manette, a Frenchman who has been wrongly imprisoned and his daughter Lucie, who marries the son of the man who imprisoned him. The later part of the story is set in the terrible events of the French Revolution, which began in 1789.

Charles Dickens wrote many famous novels, including *Nicholas Nickleby*, *David Copperfield*, *Oliver Twist* and *Great Expectations*. He died in 1870 at the age of fifty-eight, and is buried in Westminster Abbey, London.

CHAPTER ONE

Brought back to life

1775. It was the best of times. It was the worst of times. There was a king and queen on the throne of France and a king and queen on the throne of England. It was a time of hope and a time of despair.

One dark November night, an elderly man by the name of Mr Jarvis Lorry was travelling from London to Dover on the mail coach. A man on horseback caught up with the coach and gave him this message: "*Wait at Dover for Mademoiselle.*"

'Is there any reply, sir?' the messenger asked.

'Yes,' Mr Lorry replied. 'My answer is this: "*brought back to life.*"'

As the coach lumbered on through the damp mist, everybody had the same thought: it was a very strange reply indeed.

Mr Lorry sat thinking about the bank where he worked – Tellson's. But he also pictured in his mind a man of about forty-five, thin and white-haired. As they came into Dover, he looked at the rising sun and said out loud, 'Eighteen years! Oh, God, the poor man has been buried alive for eighteen years!'

Towards evening, as Mr Lorry was waiting for dinner at his inn, the waiter announced that Miss Manette had arrived from London and was ready to speak to him. Mr Lorry found her sitting in her room by the light of two

candles. She was a short, slim woman with thick golden hair and blue eyes.

'Sir,' she began, 'I believe there are things I should know about my poor father... so long dead.'

'This is very difficult...' Mr Lorry replied, 'what if he had *not* died, Miss Manette...? What if...?'

Miss Manette gasped and knelt at his feet, her face full of pain and horror. 'Oh sir, tell me the truth!' she cried.

'Your father has been found,' Mr Lorry said. 'He is alive, although greatly changed. He has been taken to the house of an old servant in Paris. That is where we are going tomorrow. You shall bring him back to life, Miss Manette.'

She shivered. 'It will be his ghost,' she whispered. 'Not him.'

'He has been found under another name,' Mr Lorry finished. 'He forgot his own a long time ago. We should bring him back to England for a while.'

Miss Manette clutched his arm and fell silent, so silent that Mr Lorry called out for help. A wild-looking woman with red hair, wearing a big bonnet, rushed into the room.

'You have frightened her to death!' she shouted at Mr Lorry.

***

In a part of Paris, known as Saint Antoine, a cask of wine had been broken outside a wine shop. Red wine spilled onto the street and people left their work to drink what they could. It was the poorest part of Paris. Hunger was found in every house and in every dirty, twisting street.

The keeper of the wine shop, a man called Defarge, was watching from his doorway. He was a short and strong man of about thirty. He wore no coat although it was cold. At the wine counter sat his wife, wrapped in fur, a shawl around her head. When she had finished cleaning her teeth with a toothpick, she took up her knitting again.

As Defarge stepped back into his shop, he saw Mr Lorry and Miss Manette, seated in the corner. He asked them to follow him to one of the houses at the back of his shop. Once inside, they climbed a steep staircase.

'Is he alone?' Mr Lorry asked Defarge. He whispered so that Miss Manette would not hear him.

'Yes, he's always alone,' he replied.

As they reached the attic of the house, Defarge took out a key.

'Is it necessary to lock him in?' Mr Lorry asked.

'Yes,' Defarge whispered. 'He's been locked up so long that if his door was left open, he'd die of fear.' He knocked on the door three times, and turned the key in the lock.

The attic was dark, although some light came from a trapdoor in the roof. In this dim light sat a white-haired man, stooping forward and making shoes.

'You're still at work, I see?' Defarge asked.

'Yes, I am working,' the old man replied. His voice was weak, like the voice of somebody who has been alone for a long time.

Defarge opened the window a little more. The man could be seen clearly now. He had a long white beard and his face was haggard and hollow-cheeked. His body was thin and wrinkled under his ragged shirt, which was as yellow as his face.

'We've got a visitor,' Defarge went on. 'Tell him your name.'

'One hundred and five, North Tower,' the man replied. He bent over his shoes once more.

'Do you remember me, Doctor Manette?' Mr Lorry asked. 'I used to be your banker.'

The old man's eyes clouded over. Miss Manette came closer and held out her arms to him. As he reached for his shoemaker's knife, he caught sight of her dress. She clasped him to her, weeping.

'Who are you?' he asked.

Miss Manette sat down on the bench next to him, her golden hair falling down. Doctor Manette put down his knife and opened a dirty rag hanging around his neck. Inside were strands of golden hair.

'Your hair is the same colour as my wife's,' he whispered. 'This hair was on my shoulder... the night... the night I was taken... But you cannot be her. You are too young. What is your name, my angel?'

'Oh, sir, I shall tell you another time,' Miss Manette said. 'I have come to take you with me to England, for France has been unkind to you. And then you can ask me my name.'

And that night, they left Paris for the long, cold journey back to England.

CHAPTER TWO

The Trial

Five years later, in 1780, a court case was being heard in London. The prisoner was a gentleman of about twenty-five, sunburnt and dark-eyed. His long dark hair was tied back with a ribbon. He bowed to the Judge and stood silent.

His name was Charles Darnay.

He had pleaded Not Guilty to a charge of treason – of spying for the king of France. And the punishment for treason was death.

Among the witnesses in court were Miss Manette, her father and Mr Lorry, who was the first to be questioned.

'Yes,' Mr Lorry said. 'I travelled across the Channel to Dover with the prisoner five years ago; but we hardly spoke.'

'Yes,' Lucie Manette said in her turn. 'Five years ago, I travelled with the gentleman… with the prisoner… across the Channel to Dover. He was very kind to my father.'

'Yes,' Doctor Manette said. 'I have seen the prisoner before, when he called at my house. But I cannot remember him on that journey from France.'

Another witness was called. He said that he had seen the prisoner waiting at an inn on the Dover road, five years before – and acting suspiciously. One of the barristers, Sidney Carton, took off his wig and asked, 'Can you see the likeness between the prisoner and myself? Can you really be sure that you saw the prisoner that night?'

The witness shook his head. And, because of this, Charles Darnay was found Not Guilty. As he was leaving the court, Carton spoke to him.

'You look faint, sir,' he said. 'Come and dine with me. This is a strange chance that has thrown us together today.'

They dined and drank good wine, and raised their glasses in a toast to Lucie Manette.

'Is it not worth being tried in court just to be the object of such kindness?' Carton asked. He paused. 'Do you think that I like you, Darnay?'

'No, I do not think that you do,' Darnay replied. 'And I think you have been drinking too much, sir. Goodnight to you.'

When Carton was alone, he looked at himself in the mirror. 'If I changed places with Darnay, would Miss Manette look at *me* with those blue eyes?' he asked himself. 'Be honest, Sidney, you are jealous of the man!'

***

Doctor Manette and his daughter lived in a quiet street of London. Four months after Darnay's trial, when most had forgotten all about it, Mr Lorry was on his way to lunch there.

It was a fine Sunday afternoon. As he waited for Lucie and her father to return from their walk, he noticed, in one of the rooms, the shoemaker's bench and tools.

'I wonder why he keeps that reminder of his sufferings?' he asked aloud.

'And why are you wondering that?' a voice asked. It was Miss Pross, the woman with the red hair whom he had first met at the Dover inn.

'How are you?' he asked.

'I'm very much put out,' she replied, 'by all the people who keep coming to the house now, ever since you brought her father back to life. I've lived with Lucie since she was ten years old. I can find no fault with her father. It's the others who want to take her away from me. I mean Mr Carton and Mr Darnay. But *no* man is good enough to marry her.'

'Does the doctor ever talk to Lucie about the shoemaking time?' Mr Lorry asked.

'Never,' she replied.

'Do you think he has any idea of who put him in prison?'

'I think so,' Miss Pross said. 'But it's better not to talk about it. Sometimes, he gets up in the dead of night and walks up and down in his room. And she always goes to walk with him.'

That evening brought two visitors – Charles Darnay and Sidney Carton. And it also brought a terrible storm. Thunder roared and lightning flashed until the great bell of Saint Paul's struck midnight.

'What a night!' said Mr Lorry, 'almost the sort of night that brings the dead from their graves.'

CHAPTER THREE

Death in the Countryside

Meanwhile, in France, the Marquis d'Evremonde, a French nobleman, was travelling from Paris to his country house. He was a man of about sixty, with a fine, but cruel, face. Every fortnight, he came to Paris to attend the parties of other great lords.

His coachman drove so fast that people screamed and scattered in the streets. As they came round a corner by a village fountain, the horses reared and stopped. A man picked up a child from under the horses' feet.

'Dead!' he shrieked.

The people stood, silent and watching, as the Marquis took out his purse.

'Why can you people not look after your children?' he asked. 'You may have injured my horses.' He threw down a coin. 'Give the man that!'

A dark-haired man made his way through the crowd to comfort the weeping father. 'Be brave,' he said, 'it's better for your poor little son to die than to live this terrible life.'

The marquis smiled. 'You are a sensible man,' he said. 'What is your name?'

'Defarge.'

'Then take this,' the marquis said, throwing down another coin. He signalled the coachman to drive on. And as they did so, the coin flew through the air and landed on the floor of the coach. 'You dogs!' the marquis muttered. 'I would like to exterminate you *all* from the earth.'

The carriage clattered through the countryside, and into a village at the bottom of a hill. Some of the villagers were talking by the water fountain, grumbling about the money they had to pay in taxes.

As his carriage slowed down by the fountain, the Marquis spoke to one of the men standing there. 'I passed you on the road just now.' he said. 'Why were you staring at my carriage?'

'There was a man, my lord, hanging underneath,' he explained.

The marquis turned to Monsieur Gabelle, the postmaster of the village – and the collector of taxes. 'If this stranger seeks lodging in the village, find out why he is here,' he ordered.

At last, the marquis arrived at his country house. It was a large stone house, with a stone terrace in front of it, decorated with stone faces of men and animals. He went straight to his apartment on the first floor of the round tower. In one of the richly furnished rooms, supper was set out for two people. Halfway through this meal, a young man was shown into the room. They did not shake hands.

'You have been a long time coming to see me, nephew,' the marquis said.

'I have been detained in London by unfortunate events,' his nephew replied. 'I hear that you were received coldly in Paris again.' He sighed. 'I believe that our name, the name of Evremonde, is the most hated in the whole of France.'

'The common people must be kept down,' his uncle muttered. 'Meanwhile, we uphold the family honour.'

'Sir,' his nephew said. 'We have done wrong, and we shall pay the price for it one day.'

'*We* have done wrong?' his uncle asked.

'Yes, you and my father,' his nephew replied. 'And it is

left me to put right a great wrong. My mother begged me with her dying breath. I want nothing of all this wealth. If I were to inherit it tomorrow, I should give it up and live elsewhere. I should live in England, where nobody knows my family name. There I am known as Charles Darnay.'

'England has become the refuge of many Frenchmen,' his uncle said. 'Have you, by chance, come across a Doctor Manette?'

'Yes,' Darnay replied. 'And I have met his daughter.'

The marquis bade his nephew goodnight. Then he walked up and down by the cool air of his bedroom window before he went to sleep. But in the morning, when the sun had stained the stone faces crimson, he was dead, a knife through his heart.

CHAPTER FOUR

A Terrible Secret

A year had gone by and Charles Darnay was now working in England as a teacher of French. He had many students and was earning a good living.

And he had fallen in love.

Darnay had loved Lucie Manette from the moment he had seen her in court. He had never heard such a sweet voice or seen such a beautiful face. He decided it was time to speak to Doctor Manette on the matter. One fine summer's day, he made his way to the house on the quiet corner. Lucie was out, but Doctor Manette was sitting in the garden.

'I love your daughter very much, sir,' he began. 'I understand how devoted she is to you. I do not want to take her from you, only to share her with you. And…' he hesitated. 'I want to tell you why I am in England, and what my real name is.'

The doctor touched his hands to Darnay's lips. 'Tell me when I ask!' he said. 'Not now.'

When Lucie returned home, she heard the faint sound of hammering in her father's bedroom. She went to his room, her heart pounding, and they walked up and down for a long time.

Sidney Carton had often been to Doctor Manette's house during the past year. But he was always sad and moody. And when he had drunk too much wine, he often walked up and down outside that quiet house until sunrise.

One day in August, he found Lucie alone, sewing. She glanced up at him. 'I fear you are not well, Mr Carton,' she said.

'The way I live does not bring good health,' he replied. Tears sprang to his eyes. 'And it is too late for me to change. I am a sad drunkard and I shall sink lower and lower in life.'

'I am sure the best part is to come, Mr Carton,' Lucie said.

They talked for a long time, until Mr Carton kissed her hand and got up to leave. 'In the hour of my death,' he said, 'I shall always remember that I have been able to talk to you. I would do anything for you, drunken wretch that I am, and for those dear to you. Try to remember the better side of my nature, Miss Manette. God bless you, and farewell!'

***

There had been early drinkers at the Defarge wine shop where Madame Defarge was taking the money in a battered bowl. Her husband had been absent for three days. At noon, he returned with a road mender, called Jacques, whom he had met outside Paris.

At a nod from Defarge, three men drinking in the bar followed them up to the attic where Doctor Manette had been living.

'Begin your story at the beginning,' Defarge told the road mender.

'I first saw the man, whose son was knocked down, a year ago,' he began, 'hanging under the carriage of the Marquis d'Evremonde. Everybody was looking for him after the murder, but he was well hidden... until now. I was out working at dusk, when I saw six soldiers bringing him over the hill to the prison in the village. The next morning, I saw him swinging there in an iron cage...'

'Go on,' said Defarge.

'They said at first he wouldn't be executed, because the death of his child had sent him mad. The king had been asked to show mercy.'

'Aye,' one of the other men said. 'It was Defarge who darted out before the king's carriage to ask for it. But the guards struck him.'

The road mender took up the story again. 'On Sunday night, when the whole village was asleep, they built a gallows, forty feet high, over the fountain. The prisoner's hanging there now, and his dead body's poisoning the water.'

'What do you say, Defarge?' one of the men asked.

'We'll destroy the marquis' house and every member of the Evremonde family!' he cried. 'Madame Defarge will keep their names where nobody will *ever* find them. She'll knit every name, stitch by stitch.'

***

The night before her marriage to Charles Darnay, Lucie was spending the evening quietly with her father. The moon shone on the garden where they sat under a tree.

'I used to look at the moon from my prison window,' he said, 'and I could not bear the light. It shone on everything I had lost.'

Lucie listened in surprise. It was the first time her father had ever spoken of his suffering.

'I thought a thousand times about the unborn child from whom I had been snatched that night,' he went on. 'I wondered if it would be a son, who would avenge his father, or a daughter who would care for me.'

The marriage day shone brightly and everybody was ready to go to church, except for Doctor Manette. He was in his room, speaking to Charles Darnay. At last, the door opened and the doctor came out, his face deathly pale. And as he took his daughter downstairs to the waiting carriage, Mr Lorry saw a look of dread pass over his friend's face.

CHAPTER FIVE

Desperate Days

Charles Darnay and Lucie Manette were married. Later that morning, Lucie waved to him from the carriage, and then she was gone. Mr Lorry, Miss Pross and the doctor were quite alone. As they went back into the cool house, Mr Lorry saw that the doctor still looked afraid.

'I think,' he whispered to Miss Pross, 'that we had better say nothing at the moment. I shall come back later to take him for a drive.'

Two hours later, when Mr Lorry returned, he found Miss Pross wringing her hands in despair. The sound of hammering could be heard upstairs.

'Oh dear, all is lost!' she cried. 'The doctor doesn't know me and he's making shoes again.'

Mr Lorry went straight to the doctor's room. The bench was turned towards the light and his head was bent over his work.

'My dear friend!' Mr Lorry called. 'Doctor Manette!'

The doctor looked at him for a moment and went back to his work. His face had taken on a haggard look – and his shirt was open at the neck as it used to be. He worked on in silence.

'Lucie must not know of this,' Mr Lorry thought. 'And neither must anybody else who knows him. Miss Pross and I will tell everybody that he is not well.'

Doctor Manette took the food and drink that was given to him; he worked every dark until dark. He refused to go

outside. But on the ninth day, Doctor Manette left his bench and sat reading at the window. His face was calm, although pale. He behaved as if nothing had happened.

'My dear friend,' Mr Lorry began. 'I hope you will advise me well. I have a friend, a friend who has a daughter, who suffered a great mental shock, nine days ago.'

'Does his daughter know?' Doctor Manette asked.

'No,' Mr Lorry replied. 'Now tell me. Why would this relapse have happened?'

Doctor Manette thought hard. 'Something must have reminded him of that terrible time,' he said, shuddering.

'Would he be relieved if he could tell his secret?' Mr Lorry asked.

'I believe so. But it may not be possible,' Doctor Manette replied.

'One more thing,' Mr Lorry said. 'This friend took up some work when he was ill. Would it be better for him to get rid of his tools of work? May I tell him that *you*, as a doctor, recommend such a thing? For his daughter's sake, Manette!'

'Very well,' the doctor replied. 'Let them be removed.'

A few days later, when Doctor Manette went to join Lucie and her husband for a visit, Mr Lorry took an axe and hacked the shoemaker's bench to pieces. Then he and Miss Pross burned it on the kitchen fire.

***

When the newly married couple came home, Sidney Carton was the first visitor to offer his congratulations. He looked as untidy and as unhappy as ever.

'I hope we may be friends,' he said quietly to Darnay.

'And I hope you will forgive my drunken behaviour in the past.'

'I declare to you, as a gentleman, that I have forgotten,' Darnay replied. 'You did me a great service that day in court.'

'I was doing my job,' Carton replied. He sighed. 'I am a good for nothing, who has never done any real good – and never will.'

Time passed by. Lucie Darnay gave birth to a daughter – also called Lucie – and Sidney Carton continued to visit the house on the corner. Uninvited, he would sit with them in the evening. But he never came drunk.

When Lucie was six years old, news came of the terrible things that were happening in France. On a mid-July night, in 1789, Mr Lorry came to the house and sat watching darkness fall. 'Our customers in France are trying to send their money to England,' he said. 'Something is *very* wrong over there, but we do not know yet what it is yet.'

CHAPTER SIX

Revolution!

Across the Channel, in that district of Paris called Saint
Antoine, people were jostling in the streets. Their knives
and bayonets gleamed in the sun. They grabbed guns,
sticks and stones. In the wine shop, Defarge was giving
orders. His wife had put aside her knitting and was
clutching an axe. A pistol and knife were tucked into her
belt, for she was to lead the women.

'To the Bastille prison!' Defarge shouted.

With a roar, the people rose to the attack. For two hours,
they fought to enter that prison, facing massive stone walls,
drawbridges, deep ditches and cannon fire. At last, when
the white flag of surrender fluttered, they entered. Defarge
found his way to one hundred and five, North Tower, and
searched the cell from top to bottom.

All day long, the poor people of Paris surged in the
streets. Tired of being poor and badly treated, they rose up
against the nobles of France, cut off their heads and
paraded them on spikes. The country house of the Marquis
d'Evremonde was burned to the ground.

And all over France, other fires burned, too.

***

During the next three years, Tellson's Bank continued to
receive news of the revolution in France from its customers
who had managed to escape. At last, Mr Lorry decided that

he must go there on business; but Charles Darnay tried to dissuade him.

'It is a long journey, sir,' he said. 'And Paris may not be safe. As a Frenchman, I have great sympathy for the poor, but…' He caught sight of a dirty, unopened envelope on the desk, so close that he could read the name: **Marquis d'Evremonde, c/o Tellson's Bank, London, England.**

His own name! The name he had confided to Doctor Manette on his marriage day.

'Nobody can tell me where this gentleman is to be found,' Mr Lorry said. 'His uncle was murdered some years ago.'

'I know the fellow,' Darnay said. 'I can deliver the letter for you.' He took himself to a quiet place and read the following:

> *"Prison of the Abbaye, Paris. June 21, 1792*
> *To the Marquis d'Evremonde*
> *I have been imprisoned in Paris. My crime?*
> *Treason against the people because I am working*
> *for a nobleman – yourself, sir. I beg you, sir, to help*
> *me, for the love of justice, for the honour of your*
> *noble name. I shall die here, soon, if you do not.*
> *Your unhappy servant, Gabelle."*

Darnay paced up and down. 'Our old and faithful servant is in danger,' he muttered to himself. 'His only crime was to collect taxes from the people. That was his job.'

'I know the bad reputation of my family,' he thought. 'But I have done nothing wrong. And neither has poor Gabelle! I shall go to Paris to plead for him.'

Darnay hurried back to Tellson's, where Mr Lorry was preparing to leave.

'I have delivered the letter to the marquis,' he said. 'Will you take his reply to a Monsieur Gabelle, a prisoner in the Abbaye? Tell him: *"He has received the letter and he will come."*

That night, the fourteenth of August, Darnay sat up late. He wrote two letters: one to Lucie, telling her not to worry, and one to Doctor Manette, confiding Lucie to his care.

The next morning, with a sinking heart, he left the house and set off for Dover. On the journey, Gabelle's words rang in his ears:

"For the love of justice and for the honour of your noble name!"

CHAPTER SEVEN

A Prisoner

The journey that Darnay made from London to Paris was full of danger. But it was not because of bad roads. No, since the king had been removed by the revolution, armed citizens guarded every town gate. They questioned every traveller. Then they sent them back or let them through.

One night, after being stopped twenty times, Darnay was sleeping in the inn of a small town. In the middle of the night, three armed men, wearing red caps, woke him up.

'As you're a nobleman, I'm going to send you on to Paris with an armed escort,' one of the men said, striking the bed with the butt of his pistol. 'Dress yourself!'

They rode through the pouring rain, until they came to the town of Beauvais, close to Paris. Darnay was alarmed. The streets were full of ragged people, who crowded around his horse.

'Down with the cursed nobleman!' they cried.

'My friends,' Darnay shouted. 'I came back to France of my own free will.'

A blacksmith ran at him, a hammer in his hand. 'You're now a traitor to France since the new law!' he cried.

The postmaster pulled Darnay into his courtyard and barred the gate.

'What law is this?' Darnay asked him.

'All property belonging to noblemen in exile is to be sold,' the postmaster explained. 'And there are rumours that all noblemen who return to France will be executed.'

That night, they rode on to Paris. The city gate was still closed, but well guarded by soldiers and citizens.

'Who is this prisoner?' a dark-haired guard demanded.

Darnay shivered at the word. The man read Gabelle's letter and took Darnay into a dark room, lit only by oil lamps – and full of drunken men.

'Citizen Defarge, is this Evremonde?' an officer asked.

'This is the man,' Defarge replied.

'Then you'll be taken to La Force prison.'

'For what offence?' Darnay demanded.

'As an exiled nobleman, you have *no* rights, Evremonde,' came the reply.

As Defarge took him away, he whispered to Darnay, 'So you married the daughter of my friend, Doctor Manette?'

'Yes,' Darnay replied. 'Will you help me?'

Defarge shook his head.

'In this prison, shall I have contact with the outside world, or am I to be buried alive?' Darnay asked. 'I *must* be able to write to Mr Lorry, of Tellson's Bank, who is also in Paris. Will you help me?'

'NO!' Defarge walked on in silence, staring straight ahead. 'I'll do nothing for you. My duty's to France and the people. I'm *their* servant, not yours.'

As they walked through the streets, only a few people stared. They were now used to seeing such sights in the streets of Paris. Even the king of France was in prison.

'I did not realise that I would be in such danger,' Darnay said to himself. 'If I had, I would not have come here.'

The prison of La Force was dark and dirty. Darnay had a single cell at the top of a flight of steps. Inside was a chair, a table and a straw mattress.

'They have left me for dead,' he thought. He walked up and down his cell. '*He* made shoes,' he muttered.

CHAPTER EIGHT

No Hope

Tellson's Bank in Paris was now situated in the former house of a great nobleman. The house had been seized by the new government, whose blue, red and white flag hung over the door. In the courtyard stood an enormous stone – a grindstone – used for sharpening knives.

Mr Lorry sat by the fire, a look of horror on his face. 'This bank is full of money and jewels and silver,' he thought to himself, 'but its owners will never claim it. Many are in prison and many have already been put to death. Thank God that nobody who is dear to me is in this terrible city!'

The bell at the great gate sounded. 'Now they are back to sharpen their weapons!' Mr Lorry thought.

But no crowd thronged into the courtyard. His door opened and in came Lucie Manette and her father.

'What has happened?' Mr Lorry cried in surprise. 'Why are you here?'

Lucie stared at him, her face pale and wild. 'Charles,' she began. 'Charles is here, in Paris, in La Force prison. We do not know why.'

As they spoke, loud voices could be heard in the courtyard below. Mr Lorry begged Lucie to go into a back room. When she had gone, he and Doctor Manette looked down from the window.

Forty or fifty people had gathered in the courtyard, all wild and smeared with blood. Two men turned the handle of the grindstone. Women held wine to their lips as they worked, their rags covered with ribbons and lace plundered from the rich. They sharpened blood-stained hatchets, knives, bayonets and swords.

'They are murdering some of the prisoners,' Mr Lorry whispered in horror. 'You must make yourself known to these devils, Doctor Manette, and get yourself taken to La Force. They will not harm you, because you were once a prisoner of the Bastille; but it may be too late to save Charles!'

Doctor Manette hurried to the courtyard, and the crowd carried him off to the prison, promising to help him. By noon the next day, he had still not returned. Mr Lorry moved Lucie and her child to safe lodgings around the corner.

At last, long after dark, Mr Lorry heard footsteps on the stairs. Defarge appeared in the doorway. He handed Mr Lorry a scrap of paper, on which Doctor Manette had scribbled: *"Charles is alive. Let Defarge give Lucie a letter from him."*

Madame Defarge, who was waiting downstairs, insisted on going with them to Lucie's lodgings. Lucie kissed Defarge's hand as he gave her the letter, little knowing what murder it had carried out during the night.

Then she wept as she read: *"Dearest – be brave. I am well, and your father has influence. Kiss our child for me."*

Lucie stooped to kiss one of Madame Defarge's hands as she knitted. 'Will you help my husband if you can?' she asked. 'As a wife and mother, I beg you.'

'I've known wives and mothers who've seen their husbands and fathers put in prison,' Madame Defarge replied. 'I've seen women suffer all their lives from hunger and sickness and misery. So why should the suffering of one person mean anything to me now?'

And with those words, she and her husband left. Mr Lorry raised Lucie to her feet. 'Courage, my child,' he said.

'That dreadful woman has cast a shadow over me,' Lucie whispered.

Four days later, Doctor Manette brought the news to Lucie. Charles Darnay – the Marquis d'Evremonde – would remain in prison, but guarded well.

Thus began their new life in Paris. Doctor Manette was allowed to visit his son-in-law every week. His old suffering had been replaced by a new strength and pride. *He* would free Charles.

There was a small window in the prison, where Charles could sometimes look down into the street. Lucie went there every day, whatever the weather, and waited for two hours. A woodcutter, who lived in a shack under the prison walls, watched her – and reported back to Madame Defarge.

The King was tried and beheaded. France was now a republic with a new motto: *Liberty, Equality and Fraternity*. Men and women by law called each other citizen and citizeness. And one new face was seen more than any on the streets of Paris: the guillotine.

'The best cure for a headache!' the citizens joked.

Every day, the carts full of noblemen and women rumbled to the guillotine. And for one year and three months, Lucie was never sure if it would cut off her husband's head.

At last, one December day of snow, Charles Darnay was called to trial. Every ruffian of Paris was there to watch. The women, including Madame Defarge, knitted as they listened.

'Take off his head!' they shouted.

Darnay explained how he had given up his title, worked for his living and had married in England, and how he had come back to France to save his servant's life. Doctor Manette said that Darnay was a good husband and father and had always been loyal to France.

'He has no sympathy for the English king,' he explained. 'His government once tried him for treason.'

Charles Darnay was set free.

But Lucie still trembled with fear. The dreadful carts still rumbled in the streets to the guillotine. Fear and distrust filled everybody's hearts and minds, especially Lucie's.

'I *have* saved him, dear child,' her father said.

That night, a knock came at the door. When Doctor Manette took the lamp and opened it, four rough men in red caps, armed with pistols, entered the room. They surrounded Darnay, where he stood with his wife and child clinging to him.

'The Citizen Evremonde, also called Darnay!' one of the men shouted.

'Who seeks him?' Darnay asked.

'I seek him,' the man said. 'Ah, I know you, Evremonde. I saw you at the tribunal today. You're now a prisoner of the republic – *again*.'

Doctor Manette caught hold of the man's rough woollen shirt. 'How can this have happened?' he asked.

'The Citizen Evremonde has been denounced by Citizen and Citizeness Defarge,' the man replied. 'And one other person.'

'Who is that?' the Doctor begged.

One of the other men rubbed his beard and looked at the doctor strangely. 'You'll know the answer tomorrow,' he replied.

CHAPTER NINE

The Secret Letter

Sidney Carton had arrived in France. He came to speak to
Mr Lorry, bringing with him a man whom he had just met
in the street – Miss Pross' brother. 'I have bad news for
you, sir,' Carton said. 'Darnay has been arrested again.'

'But I only left him two hours ago!' Mr Lorry cried.
'Can you do anything to help?'

Carton glared at the man with him. 'This man is a spy,'
he said, 'although his sister does not know it. He was
behind Darnay's trial all those years ago, when he worked
for the English government. Now he works for the French
Republic at the prison. But if Defarge knew that he once
spied on him....'

'What do you want?' the spy asked, trembling.

'If the trial goes badly for Darnay tomorrow, you must
arrange for me to see him once,' Carton said.

Mr Lorry's face fell. 'Seeing Darnay will not help him,'
When the spy had left, he gazed into the fire, crying.

Carton took his hand. 'Do not tell Lucie,' he said. 'She
would want to go with me, and they would not let her.'
Sidney Carton sighed as he spoke, standing by the fire in
his white riding-coat and boots, his long brown hair
hanging loose around his face.

'I have done all I can here,' Mr Lorry said. 'I have my
pass that will allow me to leave Paris. Now I must say
goodbye to Lucie and her child.'

'You have done much to help others in your long life,'

Carton said. 'I have earned the love and respect of nobody. *Nobody* will remember me!' He helped Mr Lorry to put on his coat. 'May I walk with you to her gate?'

Carton left Mr Lorry there and hurried on. It was ten o'clock when he stood in front of the prison of La Force. The woodcutter was smoking his pipe.

'How goes the republic, Citizen?' Carton asked him.

'You mean, how goes the guillotine?' the man laughed. 'Sixty-three heads rolled today. We'll soon reach a hundred. Have you seen her at work?'

'Never,' Carton said.

The next morning, the charge against Charles Darnay was read out in court:

"Charles Evremonde, called Darnay. Released yesterday. Re-accused and retaken yesterday. Denounced enemy of the French Republic. Denounced by Ernest Defarge, Therese Defarge and Doctor Alexandre Manette."

There was uproar. Doctor Manette, pale and trembling, rose to his feet. 'I protest!' he said. 'Who says I denounce the husband of my dear daughter?'

The president of the tribunal rang his bell for order. 'Even if the Republic of France demands the sacrifice of your child, your duty would be to sacrifice her. Listen to what is to follow. And stay silent!'

Doctor Manette sat down again, pulling Lucie closer to him, as Defarge came into court.

'Inform us what you did on the day you broke into the Bastille prison, Citizen Defarge,' the President said.

'I went to one hundred and five, North Tower, where Doctor Manette had been imprisoned for many years,' Defarge replied. 'Inside the chimney, I found a letter. I can confirm that the handwriting's that of Doctor Manette.'

The letter was read as follows:

"I, Alexandre Manette, doctor of the village of Beauvais, write this in 1767, during the tenth year of my captivity. I have little hope left now. This is my story....

One September night, in the year 1757, I was walking by the river Seine in Paris, when a carriage came alongside me. Two gentlemen, wrapped in cloaks, and armed, asked me to go with them. They knew of my skill as a doctor.

We left Paris and came to a house in the countryside. I was taken to a bedchamber, where a young woman lay. She had a high fever and was tied to the bed with a scarf initialled E. and a coat of arms. She called out for her husband and her brother.

In the stable was another patient – a boy lying in the hay store. I could see that he was dying from a stab wound.

'Have you seen my sister here, doctor?' he gasped. 'She was married, but they forced her husband to let them... have their pleasure with her. I sent my other sister to a place of safety and tracked them here, sword in my hand.' He tried to sit up, pointing to one of the gentlemen who had brought me there. 'Evremonde,' he said, 'I mark this cross of blood upon you and your brother. You must answer for the wrong you have done.'

Then he died. And a week later, so did his sister. I left those brothers without a word. But I decided to write to a government minister, stating what had happened. When I was finishing my letter, a young lady asked to see me. She said she was the wife of the Marquis d'Evremonde – the elder brother. She knew her husband's part in the cruel story, although she did not know that the girl was dead. She pointed to her young son in the carriage and wept. 'For little Charles' sake, I shall do all I can to make up for my husband's behaviour,' she said.

I delivered my letter the next day. That night, my servant Defarge, showed a man dressed in black into my room where I was sitting with my wife. He said it was an urgent case. The Evremonde brothers were waiting outside in a carriage. They burned my letter in front of me and brought me here, to this prison – to my grave.

I, Alexandre Manette, in my agony, denounce the family of Evremonde."

A terrible sound rose from the crowd when this document was finished – a cry for blood of the Evremonde family.

'See if you can save him now, my doctor!' Madame Defarge muttered.

The verdict was simple and terrible to hear: The Marquis d'Evremonde, known as Charles Darnay, was sentenced to die on the guillotine the next day.

Sidney Carton went straight from the court to the wine shop in Saint Antoine. There he bought a drink and raised his glass to the French Republic.

Madame Defarge glared at him. 'He looks like Evremonde,' she muttered to the men around her. Then she turned to her husband. 'You'd rescue him from prison if you could, wouldn't you?' she asked.

'No, I wouldn't,' her husband protested. 'But I wouldn't seek to exterminate his entire family.'

'Listen,' Madame Defarge whispered to the men. 'Listen to the secret I told my husband when he came home from the Bastille with that letter. That dying boy in the stables was my brother. That dying girl was my sister. *I* was the sister he sent away to safety.'

'It is so,' Defarge said.

'Then don't tell me to stop,' his wife spat.

CHAPTER TEN

Number Twenty-three

When Carton returned to Mr Lorry's rooms, he found him pacing up and down as he waited for Doctor Manette. And when the doctor came though the door at midnight, his face told them there was no hope.

'Where is my bench?' he asked. 'I must finish those shoes.'

'The last chance is gone,' Carton said. He took some papers from his pocket. 'Keep these safe, sir. Here is my pass to leave Paris tomorrow, and Doctor Manette's. It will allow him to leave with Lucie and the child.'

'Are they in danger?' Mr Lorry asked.

'Yes, great danger,' Carton replied. 'You remember that I have one last visit to Darnay? Everything depends on you, Mr Lorry. You must leave at two o'clock tomorrow afternoon, as soon as I return to the carriage. Do as I say, or we shall *all* die.'

'I shall play my part faithfully,' Mr Lorry said.

'And I hope to do mine,' Carton replied.

***

Charles Darnay, alone in his cell, knew that nobody could save him now. When he had written his farewell letters, he lay down on his straw bed.

'I am done with this world now,' he thought.

The next morning, he paced up and down, until he heard

footsteps in the passage and a key turning in the lock.

It was Sidney Carton.

'Are you… a prisoner here?' Darnay asked him.

'No,' Carton replied. 'I have no time to explain. Now, take off your boots and put on mine. Quickly!'

'Carton, there is no escape from this place,' Darnay said. 'You will only die with me.'

'I am not asking you to escape *with* me,' he replied. 'Put on my cloak and take that ribbon from your hair.'

Darnay did as Carton commanded. 'What is that strange… smell?' he asked. As he spoke, his eyes closed and he slipped to the floor. Carton sent for the guards at once.

'Sidney Carton is overcome with grief! Take him out to his carriage,' he ordered.

The door closed and Carton was left alone. Nobody raised the alarm and he breathed more freely as he waited. As soon as the clock struck two, his door opened and a gaoler said, 'Follow me, Evremonde!'

***

The same shadows falling on the prison were also falling on a carriage slowing down at the gates of Paris. The guards inspected the passes of its occupants, who lay asleep or weeping: Mr Lorry, Doctor Manette, Lucie, little Lucie and Sidney Carton. Then they let it pass. The carriage clattered out into the silent countryside. And only the wild wind rushed after them.

At the same time, Madame Defarge was holding a meeting in the woodcutter's house by the prison.

'The Evremonde family must *all* be wiped out,' she shouted. 'The wife and the child must follow him to the guillotine. I can't trust my husband in this matter. He's too fond of the doctor.' She called to the woodcutter. 'Are you ready to bear witness that his wife stood by the prison window every day, signalling to her husband?'

The woodcutter touched his red cap and nodded. Then he hurried to watch the three o'clock executions.

'I'll go for her now,' Madame Defarge said. 'But I'll be at the guillotine before the carts arrive. We'll denounce her tonight.'

Madame Defarge had no pity. She did not care that an innocent man should die for the sins of his family. She walked on in her ragged dress and red cap, a pistol and dagger under her clothes.

Miss Pross was preparing to leave by a later carriage. Suddenly, she cried out because Madame Defarge was standing in the room.

'The wife of Evremonde, where is she?' she demanded in French.

'You look like the devil's wife,' Miss Pross replied in English, 'but you won't get the better of me.'

Neither understood the other's words, but they understood the sense of them.

'I've been in the streets since the first day of the revolution!' Madame Defarge shouted. 'I'll tear you to pieces if you don't move from that door.'

As she ran forward, Miss Pross caught her round the waist. There was a blinding flash as Madame Defarge reached for her pistol – and slumped to the floor. Miss Pross locked the door and hurried away, dropping the key into the river as she went. She did not hear the carts rumbling to the guillotine – for, in that crack of the pistol, she had become quite deaf.

The clocks are striking three. The chairs by the guillotine are full of women, busy with their knitting – apart from one – Madame Defarge.

'She's never missed an execution before,' one of the women says.

The supposed Evremonde gets down from the cart.

'Keep your eyes on me, child,' he whispers to a young girl next to him in the line.

They stand together.

'Is the moment come?' she asks at last.

'Yes,' Carton replies. He kisses her and she is gone. Twenty-two, the knitting women count.

'I am the resurrection and the life,' Sidney Carton thinks.

Number twenty-three.

He climbs the steps to the guillotine. The crowd has never seen such peace on the face of a man going to his death. And Sidney Carton is heard to whisper at the foot of the scaffold these words:

'It is a far, far better thing that I do, than I have ever done; it is a far, far better rest that I go to than I have ever known.'

WITHDRAWN FROM STOCK